THIS BOOK
BELONGS TO

_____

_____

A LITTLE OWL BOOK

Snow White and the Seven Dwarfs

retold by Glynis Langley
illustrated by Annabel Spenceley

WORLD

Once upon a time a baby girl was born to the King and Queen of a faraway land. She was a beautiful child, with skin as white as snow, hair as black as ebony, and lips as red as blood. Most important though, she had a kind heart and a loving nature. The child was called Snow White.

Sadly, the Queen died, and Snow White's father, the King, took a new bride. But this time his Queen was a wicked woman, with evil ways and a cold heart. Her dearest possession was a magic mirror, which constantly assured her of her great beauty.

She would always ask the mirror the same question:

> *Mirror, mirror, on the wall,*
> *Who is the fairest of them all?*

And the mirror would always give her the answer she wanted.
Until, one day . . .

The wicked Queen asked the mirror the usual question, but
this time it replied:

> *Oh Lady Queen, thou still art fair,*
> *But none to Snow White can compare.*

The wicked Queen flew into a rage, and immediately called
the palace huntsman to her chamber.

She ordered the huntsman to take Snow White into the forest and slay her. The huntsman was deeply saddened by her words, but he did not dare to argue with the evil Queen. He called Snow White to his side, and asked her to go with him on his next hunting trip.

But the huntsman had no intention of killing Snow White. He loved her as everyone in the palace loved her, and as soon as they were deep in the woods he told her of the wicked Queen's words, and made her promise to run far away, where the Queen would never find her. Then, with a heavy heart, he left Snow White in the woods and returned to the palace.

Snow White was very frightened. She had never been alone before in the woods, and she did not know which way to turn. At last she found a woodland path, and she followed it through the trees until she came to a neat little house in a quiet clearing.

There was no reply to Snow White's timid knock, so she shyly ventured inside. Everything inside the house was tiny. There was a tiny table, with seven tiny chairs, and it was set with seven tiny plates and seven tiny mugs. Snow White noticed that the tablecloth was frayed and torn, and that there were cobwebs in the corner of the room.

Snow White thought it was rather sad that such a pretty house should be so untidy, and she immediately set to work mending the tablecloth, washing the dishes, sweeping the floor, and polishing the furniture. Before long the little room was spotlessly clean. Then, after all her hard work, Snow White felt rather tired.

She climbed some wooden steps to the attic bedroom, in which seven tiny beds lay side by side along the wall. Snow White lay down across all seven beds, and she had hardly closed her eyes before she fell fast asleep. It grew quite dark, and Snow White was still sleeping soundly when the seven dwarfs who lived in the house returned from their day's work.

The seven dwarfs were astonished to find their little house looking so clean and tidy, and they were even more astonished to find the beautiful Snow White asleep on their beds. The seven little men tiptoed up to her and whispered to each other: "Who can she be?" At last Snow White woke up.

Snow White stared in surprise at the seven little men, but she didn't feel afraid of them, because they looked so kind. "My name is Snow White," she told them. "What are your names?" A little man with bright red hair was the first to answer her. "I am Sunday," he said, "and these are my brothers: Monday, Tuesday, Wednesday, Thursday, Friday and Saturday."

Snow White told them the sad story of how the wicked Queen had wanted her to be killed, and how the huntsman had saved her life. When she had finished the story they begged her to stay with them in their little house.

So Snow White lived happily in the house of the seven dwarfs. She cooked delicious meals for them, and she washed and mended their clothes. Soon all the animals and birds of the woodland came to visit her, and she grew to love them all dearly.

Every morning she would stand happily at the door of the house and wave to the seven dwarfs as they went off to their day's work in the gold mines. And every evening she would be at the door again, to welcome them home.

Back at the castle, the wicked Queen had not consulted her mirror for some weeks, secure in the knowledge of Snow White's death, and feeling sure that she already knew its reply. One day, however, she decided that she would like to be flattered once more, and she asked:

> *Mirror, mirror, on the wall,*
> *Who is the fairest of them all?*

Imagine the wicked Queen's fury when she heard its reply . . .
Oh Lady Queen, thou still art fair,
But none to Snow White can compare,
Deep within the forest glen,
She dwells with seven little men.

The evil Queen immediately devised a plan. This time she determined that she would kill the girl herself. She disguised herself as an old beggar woman, and set off for the little house, carrying a basket of apples. The shining red fruit looked delicious, but one of the apples was full of deadly poison.

She knocked at the door of the house, and offered Snow White the poisoned apple. Snow White hesitated, because the dwarfs had warned her that she should never open the door and talk to strangers. But the old woman pleaded with her, and said: "I have walked over hills and dales to bring this fruit to you."

The kind-hearted Snow White, not wishing to offend an old woman, took the apple. But at the very first bite she gasped and fell to the floor. It was hours later when the dwarfs found her, as they returned from the gold mines. Her skin was warm, and somehow they knew she was not dead. But all their efforts failed to awaken her.

All was sadness in the house and in the woodland. The dwarfs placed Snow White in a coffin of glass and laid it in a shady spot beneath the trees, and all the woodland animals and birds would visit the beautiful girl, who slumbered on in her deep deep sleep.

Many months passed, until one day a Prince came riding by. He fell in love with the beautiful girl in the glass coffin, and begged the dwarfs to let him carry her back to his home. The dwarfs were sad at the thought, but they knew he loved her, and at last they agreed. But then a wonderful thing happened. . . .

The prince bent to lift up the coffin, and the sudden jolt of movement dislodged the piece of apple from Snow White's throat. The poison was gone at last, and Snow White opened her eyes and smiled at them all. There was great joy in the woodland, and Snow White fell in love with the handsome Prince who had saved her.

Soon they were married, and they went to live in the Prince's palace on the other side of the forest. But Snow White never forgot her life in the little woodland house, with the animals and birds she loved so well. And she never forgot those seven little men: Sunday, Monday, Tuesday, Wednesday, Thursday, Friday and Saturday, the seven dwarfs.